A Bit More
BERT

ALLAN AHLBERG & RAYMOND BRIGGS

FARRAR, STRAUS AND GIROUX   NEW YORK

Printed in Italy
First published in Great Britain by Viking Books, 2002
First American edition, 2002
1 3 5 7 9 10 8 6 4 2
Library of Congress Cataloging-in-Publication Data
Ahlberg, Allan
    A bit more bert / Allan Ahlberg & Raymond Briggs.
      p. cm.
    Summary: Bert receives a disastrous haircut, loses his dog,
and discovers that there are many other Berts in the world.
    ISBN 0-374-32489-1
    [1. Humorous stories.] I. Briggs, Raymond. II. Title.

PZ.A2688 Bi 2002
[E]–dc21
                                                    2001059777

CHAPTER ONE

Bert's Dog

Bert has a dog.
Here he is.
Do you like him?

Bert loves his dog.
He buys him biscuits.

BONY
BITS

He takes him for walks.
He calls him . . . Bert.

"Here, Bert!" says Bert.

CHAPTER TWO

Bert's Haircut

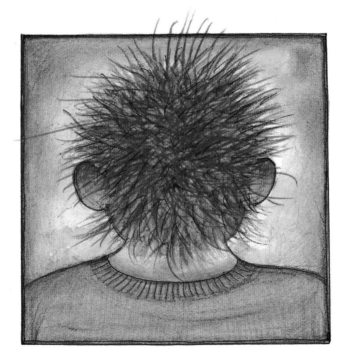

Bert's hair is too long.
He needs a haircut.
The hairdresser is shut.
Can you help?

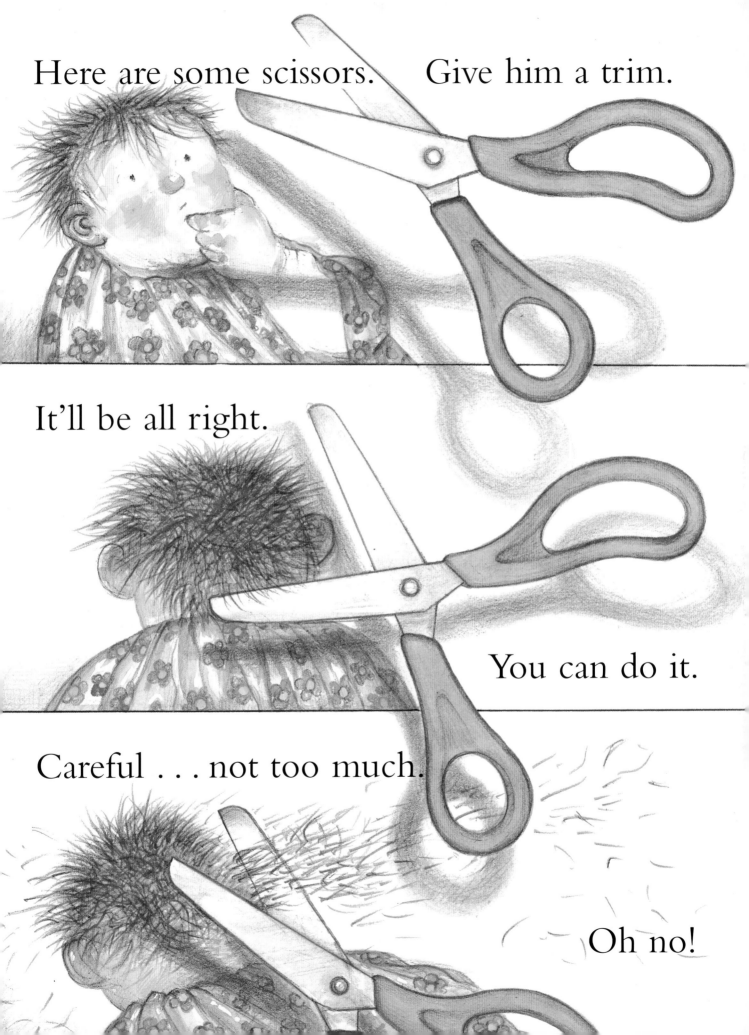

Poor Bert . . . *bald* Bert.

CHAPTER THREE

Bert's Mother

Bert has a mother.
Here she is.
Her name is Grandma Bert.

Grandma Bert loves Bert.
She loves cooking him things
and telling him what to do.

"Drive carefully, Bert," says Grandma Bert.

"Wipe your feet!"

"Blow your nose!"

"Eat your cabbage!"

Bert loves his mother.
He does whatever she tells him.
But—shh!—this is a secret.
He *never* eats his cabbage.

CHAPTER FOUR

Bert's Chips

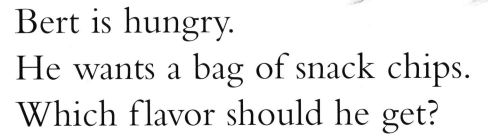

Bert is hungry.
He wants a bag of snack chips.
Which flavor should he get?

Bert shares his chips.
One for Mrs. Bert.

One for
Grandma Bert.

One for
Baby Bert.

One for
Bert the dog . . .   and one for you!

Thanks, Bert!

CHAPTER FIVE

Bert's Dog Again

Bert takes Bert for a walk.

Bert runs off.

Bert chases Bert.

Where did he go?
Let's find him.

Turn the page!

Oh no! We've lost him.

Bert looks everywhere for Bert.

He goes to the police station.

"I've lost my dog," he says.

"What's your name?" says the policeman.

"Bert," says Bert.

"What's your dog's name?"

"Bert again," says Bert.

The policeman smiles.
"That's a funny thing," he says.
"My name's Bert as well."

"And mine!" says
another policeman.

"I've got a guinea pig named Bert," says a policewoman.

"That's nothing," the sergeant says. "I've got *six* goldfish . . . all named Bert!"

Bert keeps looking for Bert.
It gets dark.
Bert goes home.

He finds Bert on the doorstep.

And Bert finds him.

Happy Berts!

CHAPTER SIX

Berts' Bedtime

It is bedtime now.
Mrs. Bert shares her
bedtime chips with Bert.
Bert the dog is in his kennel.

Bert the policeman is on his beat.

Bert the guinea pig is in his cage.

Bert and Bert and Bert
and Bert and Bert and Bert the goldfish
are in their garden pond.
There's only one thing left to say . . .

(turn the page)

"Good night, Bert!"